ANIMAL RESCUE CENTER

The Lucky Rabbit

ANIMAL
+RESCUE CENTER

Other titles in the series:

ANIMAL RESCUE CENTER

The
Lucky
Rabbit

by TINA NOLAN

This series is for my riding friend Shelley,
who cares about all animals.

tiger tales

5 River Road, Suite 128, Wilton, CT 06897
Published in the United States 2019
Originally published in Great Britain 2007
by the Little Tiger Group
Text copyright © 2007, 2019 Jenny Oldfield
Interior illustrations copyright © 2019 Artful Doodlers
Cover illustration copyright © 2019 Anna Chernyshova
Images courtesy of www.shutterstock.com
ISBN-13: 978-1-68010-125-6
ISBN-10: 1-68010-125-0
Printed in China
STP/1800/0217/1018
10 9 8 7 6 5 4 3 2 1

For more insight and activities, visit us at www.tigertalesbooks.com

Contents

ANIMAL MAGIC
RESCUE CENTER

 HOME

 ADOPT

 FRIENDS

MEET THE ANIMALS IN NEED OF A HOME!

BUN-BUN AND BELLA

What a cute pair! These two friendly and inquisitive bunnies are looking for new homes.

COCOA

Dumped next to a garbage can and left to starve, Cocoa loves to be groomed. Totally adorable!

SNOWFLAKE

A beautiful, roly-poly cat with a soft coat. She loves ball games. Are there any soccer fans out there?

SITE SEARCH

 NEWS

 HELP US

 CONTACT

 DONATE!

BILLIE AND BAILEY

Two fluffy abandoned guinea pigs. Can you give these playmates a home together?

PARKER

This handsome elderly dog loves to sleep. He's looking for a nice, quiet home.

LILY

Lily is all alone in the world. Can you give her the loving home she needs?

Chapter One
Holly's Training

"Jump, Holly, jump!" Ella stood in the yard at Animal Magic, training Holly to leap through a hoop.

Holly was the Harrisons' black-and-white Border collie pup. She raced toward the hoop, then screeched to a halt. She sat and stared at it, her head tilted to one side.

"You didn't jump," Ella said with a disappointed frown. At this rate, Holly's agility training would never take off.

"Try lowering the hoop," Ella's dad, Mark, suggested as he led Gypsy the pony out of the stables.

Clip-clop, clip-clop—Gypsy's hooves sounded hollow. Holly pricked up her ears and ran to investigate.

"Here, Holly! Good dog!" Ella called. On the list for this morning's training routine were the weave poles and seesaw, as well as the hoop.

Agility training was Ella's latest Big Idea.

"Holly has learned how to sit and do all the basics," she'd explained to her mom, dad, and brother, Caleb, at breakfast the day before. "Now I want to train her to do more complicated stuff."

Caleb had given one of his big-brother

snorts. "Ella found a website on agility training," he explained to his parents. "She was on it for hours. It shows pictures of dogs on seesaws and dogs crawling through tunnels. She figures Holly is going to be a champion!"

"Isn't she a little young?" Mom had asked, glancing at Holly curled up on her bed in the kitchen. "Don't dogs have to be fully grown before they can officially enter agility tests?"

But Ella's dad had encouraged her. "You can never start them too young, eh, Ella? For all we know, Holly might be a puppy prodigy!"

So here she was, on a cold Saturday morning in March, her red jacket zipped up to her chin, trying to persuade Holly to jump through a hoop.

"Here, Holly!" she called again. This time the puppy obeyed. She ran back to Ella and wagged her tail.

Meanwhile, Dad tied up Gypsy and went inside to muck out her stable.

Ella held the bright green hoop close to Holly's nose. "Smell this. It's made of plastic. And all you have to do is jump right through the middle!"

Holly sniffed and gave the hoop a lick.

"You—through—here!" Ella explained carefully. Then she spotted Caleb coming out of the reception area. "Hey, can you hold this for me?" she called.

Reluctantly, he came over and took the hoop from Ella. "Like this!" she told Holly.

She scrambled clumsily through it, then turned to face her. "Ta-da!"

Yip! Holly said, with an excited wag of her tail. But she didn't move.

"Terrific!" Caleb laughed. "Just like on the website—not!"

Ella's feelings were hurt. "I don't know why you're laughing," she said. "You should be helping me to train Holly, not making fun."

Caleb shrugged. "Like Mom said, she's too young for agility training, aren't you, Holls?" He leaned forward and patted her.

"You're just making excuses not to bother," Ella argued. "You won't be laughing when Holly becomes the youngest champion ever!"

Yip! Holly barked, her brown eyes sparkling.

Just then, a car turned into the yard off Main Street. A man and a girl climbed out.

"Hiya, Caleb!" the dark-haired girl called.

Ella saw her brother's face turn red. She recognized the pretty newcomer as Mia Logan—a girl in the same class as Caleb at Lakewood Middle School. "What's she doing here?" she whispered.

"The Logans are moving to Crystal Park," he hissed back. He picked up Holly and held her close as if he was trying to hide behind her. "Today, actually!"

"So this is Animal Magic?" the tall man said as he glanced at the stables, the cat area, kennels, and the porch leading into the reception area. "I hear you have a great set-up—Mia's told me all about it."

"Thanks for promising us the hay for Fern's new hutch." Mia breezed up to Caleb.

"One less thing for us to think about," Mr. Logan explained to Ella. "Moving is hectic enough, without having to remember to stock up with things like hay, so we really appreciate the help."

"Come with me," Caleb told Mia, thrusting Holly into Ella's arms and leading Mia toward the stables.

"Mia's crazy about her rabbit," Mr. Logan continued. "She can hardly stand to be separated from her. Fern gets only the best food and bedding. And we just bought her a brand-new hutch."

Ella smiled and nodded. She watched Caleb carry the overflowing bag out of the stable. "Watch out for Gypsy!" she warned.

The little chestnut pony suddenly reached out and took a mouthful of hay

from Caleb as he passed. Mia grabbed
Caleb's arm as if she was scared. Caleb's
face grew redder still.

"Here, let me," Mr. Logan said, striding across the yard to take the bag from Caleb.

"Come on, Mia, let's get a move on. There are a million and one jobs to do back at the new house."

Quickly, they thanked Caleb, put the hay in the trunk, then drove off.

"So?" Ella demanded as Mr. Logan drove off.

"So—what?" Caleb muttered, picking pieces of hay from his sleeve.

"You're blushing red—red—red!" Ella laughed.

Caleb frowned, then glared at her. "Am not!" he mumbled as he stalked off. "You stick to dog training, Ella. Concentrate on Holly, why don't you!"

Chapter Two
A Lucky Find

"Dad and I have decided to hold a spring party!" Mom announced later that morning. She stood in the reception area with Ella, Caleb, and their grandpa, Jimmy Harrison.

"Cool!" Caleb and Ella cried.

"Not next Saturday, but the one after—to celebrate Animal Magic's success," Mom explained. "And to thank everyone who has helped to make it happen over the last year."

"Great idea. We'll design an invitation and put it up on the website." Caleb got busy right away.

"Print some so we can hand them out around town." Ella couldn't wait—an Animal Magic party would be super-cool! "Jen will be back by then, so she can help us celebrate, too."

"Where is Jen?" Grandpa asked as Ella sat with Caleb to work on the invitations.

"She's taking a class," Mom replied. "She wants to update her knowledge on small animal care."

"Ella, how did you do with Holly this morning?" Dad interrupted as he came in from the yard. "Did she eventually jump through the hoop?"

Holly sat on her bed, ears pricking up

when she heard her name.

"Ha!" Caleb grinned. "Do pigs fly?"

Mom looked out the window as a vehicle similar to Dad's own delivery van pulled off Main Street into the yard. "Mark, isn't that Stephen Jennings? I wonder what he's doing here."

They didn't have to wait long to find out. They saw Dad's coworker jump out of his van, carrying what looked like an injured dog wrapped in a blanket.

Ella ran out with her mom and dad to help. She held the door while Stephen carried the dog into the reception area.

"I found her in the parking lot at the back of the big chocolate factory in Crystal Park," Stephen explained. "I was delivering packages when I spotted her lying next to a garbage can."

"Thanks for bringing her in," Dad said, watching anxiously as Mom led the way into an examination room and asked Stephen to place the dog on the table.

Ella gasped when she saw the condition that the poor dog was in. She was a dark brown cross-breed without a collar, so thin that you could see her ribs, with a big cut across the pad of her front paw. Her eyes were glazed over.

"This looks serious," Mom said
quietly, glancing up at Dad with a
worried look in her eye.

"Ella, run to the house and get my
white coat. Check that the stethoscope
is in the pocket. Mark, would you
please get the stand for a fluid drip?
Stephen, I'm sure Jimmy would take

you to the house and make you a cup of coffee, if you'd like one...."

For the next hour, Ella watched anxiously as her mom worked. Would she be able to revive the poor, starving dog and patch up the gash on her foot? She stayed in the examination room while Mom attached the drip, then stitched the wound. All the while, the patient lay with her eyes half closed.

"Ella, can you please go and get a clean blanket?" Mom would ask. Or, "Rub her head and speak softly to her while I clean the cut. That's right."

"You're going to be fine," Ella whispered to the dog. "We'll take care of you and make you better."

"Her heartbeat is stronger," Mom announced after she'd finished the sutures. "I've given her an injection of antibiotics to clear up any infection."

"Will she be okay?" Ella breathed. The dog's eyes were fully open now, and she was trying to lift her head. Mom nodded. "Let's hope so. I can only say one thing for certain—she wouldn't have made it through another night if Stephen hadn't brought her in."

"Did I hear my name being mentioned?" Stephen asked as Caleb showed him into the examination room.

"Mom says you're a hero—you saved her life!" Ella exclaimed.

"Did I really?" Stephen beamed. "That's good to hear."

"She's not microchipped, so as soon as she's well enough, we'll put her on our website for someone to adopt," Ella rushed on. "She needs a name. What would you like to call her?"

"Me?" Stephen blushed. He seemed happy to be asked. "Well, I suppose since I found her at the chocolate factory, and because she's a beautiful dark brown color, we could call her Cocoa."

"Cool," Caleb agreed.

Ella grinned. She rubbed the patient's soft, floppy ears. "Did you hear your new name, Cocoa? You're going to get well soon, and we're going to find you a perfect new home."

Chapter Three
Meeting Fern

As soon as Cocoa seemed to be through the worst, Ella dashed back to the house to find Holly. The puppy was at the door, waiting for her with a sad "Where have you been?" expression.

"I know—I've been gone a long time!" Ella admitted, kneeling down to give her a hug. "We had an emergency. But I'm here now. And listen, Holly, I've got another idea—I know it was hard for you to learn to jump through the hoop, so I've decided we should join an agility training club!"

Yip! Holly loved being cuddled and petted. She licked Ella's hands.

"I'm going to look on the Kennel Club website!" Ella declared. "It'll tell us where our nearest club is. There'll be a lot of other dogs learning to run through tunnels and do the weave poles. You'll be able to copy them!"

"In the meantime, has Holly had her morning walk?" Dad asked as he came downstairs into the kitchen.

"Oops—no!" Ella realized they'd all been too busy. "I'll take her now."

"Caleb's almost ready to print out the party invitations, and he wants your final approval," her dad reminded her as Ella grabbed Holly's leash and led her out of the house. "So don't be too long."

"I'll be back before you know it!" Ella called. She strode out of the yard.

"Hi, Ella! Hi, Holly!" Annie Brooks called from next door.

Holly heard Annie's voice and tugged at the leash. Together, she and Ella joined Annie, who was dressed in her favorite Animal Magic sweatshirt and jeans.

"Hi, Annie!" Ella grinned, unzipping her jacket. "Keep the Saturday after next free—we're having an Animal Magic party!" she announced. "Tell your mom and dad. Tell everybody!"

Annie nodded. "Okay, I'll mention it to the Logans. I'm going to Three Oaks Road with Mom in a minute to help them move in. Mom is Mrs. Logan's best friend."

"That's great!" Ella said, eager now to be on her way. "See you later!" She waved at Linda Brooks, who had just come out of the house, then at George Stevens, turning in to the yard at Animal Magic on his bike.

"Is Caleb here?" George yelled.

Ella nodded. At this rate she'd never get down to the riverside. "Come on,

Holls, let's go!" she said, setting off at a brisk walk.

Half an hour later, Ella was back at home. She had the next part of her day planned out, and first up was checking on the Kennel Club website for a local agility training club.

"Phone call for you," her dad said as she walked through the kitchen door. He held out the phone.

"Hi again, Ella," Annie said. "You have to come up to Three Oaks Road!"

"Hi, Annie. What's wrong? Has something happened?"

"No, nothing bad. But you totally have to come and see Fern."

"I'm a little busy. Maybe later."
Ella chose a ham, cheese, and pickle
sandwich from a plate on the table. She
took a big bite.

"But Fern is so beautiful!" Annie
exclaimed. "Ella, Mia got Fern a
big new hutch with a living area
and a separate bedroom and feeding
platform. Mr. Logan is going to build a
run in the yard. It'll be really cool!"

"Sounds good," Ella admitted.

"Better than good, Ella!" Annie was
bubbling with excitement. "This is a
rabbit mansion! And Fern is just so
adorable—you've got to come and
see!"

It was no use—Ella couldn't resist.
Quickly, she told Holly to lie in her
bed. "Give me 10 minutes," she told

Annie. "I'll be right there!"

Ella rode up to Three Oaks Road on her bike, pedaling hard up the hill and getting off outside the house where a big moving truck was parked. She took off her helmet, then stood aside as two men carried a couch down the ramp.

"Hi, Ella—you'll be so glad you came!" Annie cried, running down the driveway to meet her. "Mia's helping Fern get used to her new hutch—come and see!"

So Ella followed Annie around the side of the house into the backyard, where they found Mia kneeling by a big new two-story rabbit hutch. In her arms she held a soft, caramel-colored rabbit with long, floppy ears and big, dark eyes.

"Now Fern, this is your new home," Mia was saying. "You have a downstairs room, where you can sit and see what's going on in the yard. Then you walk up the ramp here, into your bedroom, where it's nice and cozy."

"Isn't she cute?" Annie whispered to Ella as they joined Mia and Fern. "Look at those adorable floppy ears!"

Ella smiled. She loved Fern's big, dark

eyes and her soft brown nose, her long whiskers and her drooping ears. "She looks kind of sad," she said softly.

"Fern is a dwarf lop," Mia told them, letting them pet the rabbit. "She's a year old, and she won't grow any bigger. She weighs a little more than four pounds."

"She's beautiful!" Ella sighed. "How long have you had her?"

"Since she was a baby," Mia explained. "She wasn't very well at first—the vet in Crystal Park said she hadn't been given the right food to eat at the place where we got her, so since then I've given her the best of everything—the best oats, the best hay, the best fruit and vegetables...."

"In other words, you spoil her!" Annie laughed.

"That's what Mom and Dad say," Mia

confessed with a slow smile. "But I can't help it, can I, Fern?"

"This has to be the best hutch, too!" Ella grinned as she inspected Fern's new home. "I like the bedroom—it's nice and high off the ground."

Mia nodded. "It keeps her dry, and foxes can't get near her. I've lined the floor with wood shavings and hay so she can snuggle up at night."

"Cool!" Annie was impressed.

"I've put her food bowl in the compartment next to the bedroom so she won't have far to go if she wakes up hungry. And her water bottle attaches to the wire netting. It even fits into a little padded sleeve so the water won't freeze in winter!"

"I like it!" Ella said. "I wonder if Fern

knows how lucky she is."

"Let's see," Mia said quietly, deciding that it was time to let her rabbit explore her new hutch. She asked Annie to open the door, then she placed Fern inside and closed the door behind her.

At first, Fern just crouched on the cold grass and twitched her nose. Ella noticed she was shivering. "The poor little thing's not sure what's going on," she said. "Everything is so new."

"It's okay, Fern," Mia whispered. "It's safe to take a look around."

The small rabbit blinked, then took one hop forward. She sniffed at the ground, then at the wooden ramp leading to the upper level.

"I put some chopped apple and carrots in her food bowl," Mia whispered to Ella and Annie. "I'm hoping the smell will attract her."

Sure enough, Fern placed her front paws on the ramp and sniffed the air.

"Yummy carrots!" Annie breathed. Ella willed Fern to keep going.

Hop-hop—she was halfway up the ramp.

She twitched her nose, smelling the hay in the bedroom. Hop-hop—up the ramp and out of sight.

"Yesss!" Mia, Annie, and Ella grinned happily. They heard Fern rustle through the sawdust and hay and waited for her to follow her nose, out through the bedroom door onto the feeding platform. Sure enough, a small brown nose and a pair of long whiskers soon appeared.

"Sooo sweet!" Annie whispered.

Even though it was cold and windy in Mia's yard on the hill, Ella felt a warm glow inside her. She watched Fern emerge from her bedroom, her brown eyes shining, her beautiful caramel coat gleaming in the sunlight.

As soon as Fern spotted the dish of fruit and vegetables, she dashed across the platform. Hop-hop, hop-hop. She was there and digging in, head down, with her sharp teeth chomping.

"Cute!" Ella beamed. "Thanks for inviting me, Annie. I wouldn't have missed this moving-in day for anything!"

Chapter Four
An Unhappy Bunny

"Fern's fur is pale brown—like coffee ice cream!" Ella gushed. "She has big, big brown eyes and the cutest nose…!"

"Yeah, yeah—don't go on about it," Caleb told Ella as they sat in the reception area the next morning. "I saw the rabbit myself, if you must know."

Ella looked surprised. Then she felt silly for showering Caleb with every detail of Fern's appearance. "How did you see her?"

"I was at George's house yesterday. He lives next door, remember?"

"But that doesn't explain how you actually saw Fern. She didn't escape into George's yard, did she?" Ella knew that George Stevens had a rabbit of his own who might not be too friendly toward a newcomer.

"No, don't worry," Caleb insisted. He was busy entering some new arrivals on the Animal Magic website. "Billie and Bailey—two fluffy abandoned guinea pigs...."

"So?" As usual, once Ella had sunk her teeth into a subject, she didn't let go.

"So, George and I—we happened to look over the fence while Mia's dad was building the rabbit run." Caleb concentrated on the keyboard. "Can you give these playmates a home together?" he typed.

"Oh, you just happened to look!" Ella exclaimed. "Don't tell me—you offered to lend Mr. Logan a hammer and some nails. Next thing you knew, you just happened to be having a cozy chat with Mia again!"

"Actually no," Caleb muttered.

Ella wasn't really being mean when she teased Caleb about Mia—in fact, she'd like him to have a girlfriend. And Mia Logan seemed nice, with her shiny, dark cropped hair and warm smile. "Anyway, what did you think of Fern?" Ella rubbed the top of the counter with an antiseptic wipe, ready for the next arrival. So far this morning,

they'd taken in Billie and Bailey, plus
a black dog named Parker and a white
cat named Snowflake. Poor Parker had
been left behind when his elderly owner
had moved into a nursing home, while
Snowflake had come to them from an
empty house in Ridgefield.

"Fern's sweet," Caleb said. He logged
off and stood up, heading toward the
intensive care unit, where they were
still keeping an eye on Cocoa's progress.
"But I wouldn't go over the top the way
you, Annie, and Mia do," he added as
he left.

"Hi, Mom—how's Cocoa?" Ella called
later that morning. She was in the yard

with Holly, still
teaching her
the hoop trick.
Holly had
made friends
with the plastic

hoop now. She liked to seize it between
her teeth and shake it. She yelped with
delight when Ella rolled it across the
yard. But when Ella held it and cried,
"Jump!" she still sat right down and
stared at it with a puzzled look.

"Cocoa's improving rapidly," Mom
replied. She leaned back against the
porch and took a couple breaths of fresh
air. "Nice morning," she said. "It feels
like spring is on its way."

"Jump!" Ella told Holly, holding the
hoop in position. No response. "Good—

I'm glad Cocoa's going to get better."

Mom smiled. "Before you know it, you and Holly will be taking her for walks by the river. She'll be running in and out of the fields of daffodils."

"Then we'll find her the perfect owner!" The future for the stray dog seemed bright to Ella. She glanced up as Mia Logan appeared at the gate. "Hi, Mia! Is everything all right with Fern?"

"Yes, she's fine," Mia answered. "Mom's visiting next door, so I thought I'd see what's going on around here."

Ella grinned. "Mom, this is Mia," she explained. "She just moved to Three Oaks Road."

"Ah, you're the girl with the magnificent rabbit hutch!" Mom remembered Ella telling everyone about it at breakfast. "I don't suppose you want a couple of new friends for your rabbit, do you?"

"Hey, yes—Bun-Bun and Bella!" Ella nodded, thinking of the two black-and-white rabbits in the small animals unit. "There'd be plenty of room in your new hutch."

Mia shook her head. "No, I'm sorry. Fern needs time to settle in to her new home."

She took a deep breath. "Actually, you were right, Ella. That's really why I came over," she confessed. "I put out Fern's food yesterday at lunchtime, the same as usual, and when I looked this morning, she hadn't eaten a thing."

"So you're wondering about her loss of

appetite?" Mom checked. "I'm sure it's nothing to worry about at the moment. As you said, you have to give her time to get used to her new surroundings. Remind me—when did you move her in?"

"Yesterday," Mia said quietly.

Mom smiled. "Oh, well, there's no need to worry. Just go on as you normally do—give her fresh fruit and vegetables as well as her usual feed, and change her water every day. I'm sure you know all that already."

"Thanks," Mia replied. Mom's advice seemed to have reassured her, so she turned to Ella. "Is Caleb here?" she asked. "I wanted to ask him about our science homework."

The next day was Monday, and Ella
was late for the school bus.

"No, Holls, not today!" she sighed,
as the boisterous Border collie tugged
the green hoop into the middle of the
kitchen floor. Ella grabbed her school
bag and patted the puppy good-bye.

"You forgot your party invitations!"
Ella's dad yelled after her. "I thought
you wanted to hand them out at
school."

"Oops!" She ran back to grab them.

"And your lunch box!" he added,
holding it out for her.

"Oops again!" At last she had
everything and hurried to meet the
others at the bus stop.

Soon the bus appeared around the
corner.

"How's Fern today?" she asked Mia.

"The same," came the quiet answer. "I was telling Caleb—she's still not eating, and she just kind of sits there. She doesn't want to play or anything."

"Maybe she needs a toy inside her hutch," Ella suggested, climbing onto the bus after Mia.

"I already mentioned that—she has a bunch," Caleb reported from behind. "I told Mia that she should bring Fern into Animal Magic after school today if she's still worried."

Ella nodded. Caleb had hit upon the right solution. "Mom will check her," she promised. "Yes, bring her in—that's a good idea."

Fern sat on the counter in the reception area at Animal Magic.

Her head was hunched into her shoulders, and her soft, droopy ears trailed on the shiny surface.

"Not a happy bunny," Mom agreed. She slid one hand under Fern's rear end and one under her chest, then turned her over to feel her abdomen.

"That seems okay," she reported, "and her ears and nose are clean. Her teeth are okay, too."

Mia listened carefully. "Fern's never been like this before," she told Mom, who went on examining the patient. "She's usually really lively and happy to see me. But when I got home from school today, she sat in her bedroom, moping."

Mom put Fern back down on the counter and petted her. "There are some common problems that would make a rabbit feel miserable—ear mites, for instance, or overgrown teeth."

"Oh, no!" Mia assured her. "I give Fern lots of things to chew on."

Mom nodded. "Yes, as I said— her teeth are absolutely fine. And what about her droppings? Are they normal?"

Mia nodded. "Everything's normal,

nothing's changed—except for the fact that we moved into a new house, and Fern has a new hutch."

"Which is like a palace for rabbits!" Ella broke in.

"So I really think there's nothing seriously wrong," Mom decided, giving Fern one last pet and putting her back inside the pet carrier. She saw Mia's mom finish her phone call out on the porch, then come in through the door. "You can take Fern home to her wonderful new hutch!" she announced cheerfully. "I've just been telling Mia that as far as I can tell, there's absolutely nothing to worry about."

Chapter Five

A Troubling Situation

"What's wrong, Ella?" Dad was
surprised to see her slumped in front
of the TV. "Why aren't you out with
Holly, doing your agility training?"

It was Tuesday, and Ella had been
home from school for half an hour. She
lay on the couch with Holly snuggled
beside her.

"I just called the Kennel Club and
it turns out Mom was right—puppies
have to be 15 months old before they are

allowed to enter agility competitions."

"Hmm." Her dad nodded sympathetically, then sat down on the arm of the couch.

Ella frowned as she recalled her phone conversation. "The man said Holly was way too young to even join a class."

Dad nodded again. "So? That doesn't stop you from teaching her yourself. Like we said, Holly might be a quick learner."

Yip! Holly heard her name. She pricked up her ears and scrambled down to the floor. Then she ran and dragged the green hoop from the corner of the room.

"See!" Ella's dad grinned. "She's incredibly smart."

"I know," Ella sighed. "But...."

"But nothing!" Dad cried. "Come on, girls, let's get training!"

So they went into the yard, and Dad held the hoop while Ella ran up to it and jumped through. "Like that!" she told Holly.

Yip! At last a light dawned in the puppy's eyes. She ran to the hoop and with a neat skip and a hop, she was through.

"Yesss!" Ella gave her dad a high five. "Again, Holly—again!"

"So we're having a good week." It was
Wednesday, and Caleb was putting
Cocoa on the website, along with
Parker and Snowflake, while Mom was
speaking on the phone to Jen. "I've told
you about the party a week from this
Saturday. And, yes, we've been busy
in the hospital, but Ella has still found
time to teach Holly to jump through a
hoop!"

Ella grinned. "Tell her we've moved on
to the weave poles!"

"Oh, and weave poles—whatever they
are," Mom added.

Ella took the phone from her mom.
"Hi, Jen! It's a line of poles spaced out
across the yard—I'm using Annie's

jumping poles—and Holly has to weave in and out of them as fast as she can. The trouble is, she keeps knocking them over...."

Caleb stood up from the computer. "Can I speak to her?" he asked. "Hi, Jen. How's the course?"

"Interesting," Jen said. "I'm learning a lot of new stuff."

"Mom's putting you on speakerphone. Are you doing anything about rabbits?"

"As a matter of fact, yes," Jen answered. "Why do you ask?"

"Is it normal for a rabbit to not eat its food and mope around when it's moved to new surroundings?" Caleb asked. "I have a friend whose rabbit has a new hutch. And the family has moved to a new house. Mom examined her, and she can't find anything wrong."

"But your friend is still worried?" Jen asked.

"Yes, she wasn't in school today. Her mom called the school to say she's got an upset stomach, but I was talking to Mia just yesterday, and I know she's making herself sick worrying about Fern."

"Hmm." Jen thought for a few seconds. "And the rabbit's teeth, eyes, and nose were all fine? And there's no swelling around the eyelids or head?"

"No, there's no sign of any viral infection, no problems with diarrhea," Mom added. "I think it's probably a case of the owner being overanxious, and in fact pampering Fern a little too much. My advice was to leave her alone to settle in quietly."

"Fair enough," Jen agreed. "And if all else fails, you could suggest a companion rabbit for Fern. That often does the trick."

"We already did that," Ella cut in. "Mia said no."

Jen had run out of ideas. "It sounds like you've done all you can for now. I guess you'll just have to wait and see."

"Or try again with the companion rabbit idea," Caleb muttered. "Thanks, Jen. Enjoy the course. See you on Saturday. 'Bye!"

"You know, we were wondering the other day—is Fern lonely?" Caleb said.

Ella, Annie, and Caleb had gotten off
the school bus the next day and gone
straight up Three Oaks Road to visit
Mia, who was still off from school with
an upset stomach and a headache.

They were all sitting on the grass
around Fern's hutch, but there was no
sign of Fern herself.

"She's in her bedroom," Mia had told them. "And she's hardly touched the food in her dish. I've been checking all day. And she hasn't even come down the ramp to use her new run—not once!"

They all stared at the long, empty framework of wire netting and wood, which stretched half the length of the Logans' lawn.

"Mia's making herself sick," Mrs. Logan had told Caleb, Ella, and Annie when she'd answered the door. "Not only do I have a sick rabbit on my hands, but now a daughter making herself sick with worry, too! Anyway, I'm glad you've come to cheer her up."

"...Lonely?" Mia said now. It was obvious she hadn't given this another thought. "I've had her a year, and she's never seemed lonely before."

"But rabbits like company," Caleb explained. "They often get bored when they're by themselves."

"I couldn't have another one!" Mia shook her head. "If Fern had another rabbit in her hutch and I had to feed and brush them both, she'd get jealous."

"Maybe at first," Caleb said. "But she'd soon get used to it."

"No, Fern is too special." Mia sighed. She was so worried about her beloved pet that she couldn't see that Caleb might be right.

"Anyway, Mom and Dad wouldn't let me. They already think I spend way too much time fussing over one rabbit, let alone two!"

"That's a good point," Annie admitted.

"I know what my dad was like before we got Rosie. He thought it was enough hard work taking care of Buttercup and Chance without taking on another pony."

"But that's different!" Ella objected. "We're talking about rabbits here. They're not half as much work."

"Oh, yes, they are!" Mia frowned at Ella.

"Every day I have to clean Fern's litter box and put down new bedding. And every week, I have to disinfect the hutch. Then there's the brushing and feeding, and making sure that Fern doesn't try to dig her way out of her run. Then I have to spend at least an hour every day playing with her and keeping her happy…."

"Okay, I'm sorry," Ella mumbled, realizing that she should have known better.

"...I even take Fern for walks on her leash!" Mia insisted, tears brimming up and falling down her cheeks. "When she's well enough, anyway...."

"Don't cry," Ella said, offering Mia a crumpled tissue.

Mia nodded and blew her nose. "I'm sorry. I'm just so worried about her!"

It was then that Fern decided to come out. She poked her blunt brown nose through the opening, then shuffled forward onto the feeding platform, her long ears flopping over her face. She blinked in the daylight.

"Oh, Fern, there you are!" Mia sighed. She resisted the urge to open the hutch and cuddle her. Instead, she, Caleb, Annie, and Ella watched nervously as Fern made her way toward her feeding dish. "There—nice apples—your favorite!" she said.

The little toffee-colored rabbit sniffed at the fruit. She nuzzled at the mix of loose oats and flaked, dried vegetables, edged around her dish, and took a sip of water from her bottle. Then she took one more sniff at her dish.

"Sweet apples!" Mia whispered. "Yum yum!"

But Fern seemed to shake her head.

"Oh, she's trembling, poor little thing!" Annie said.

"And she's definitely not eating," Ella added. She watched Fern lift one paw to her face and scratch beneath her ear.

Even this seemed like too much effort and she soon gave up, shuffling back into the darkness and silence of her room.

"Fern's not doing well!" Annie said to Ella as they left the house ahead of Caleb, who'd stayed behind to catch Mia up on the schoolwork she'd missed. The two girls walked down the hill toward Main Street.

"I know!" Ella agreed. "But the trouble is that Mom, Jen, Caleb, and I can't think of a single thing to do to help her!"

Chapter Six
A Good Day

"Thirty-five seconds!" Ella clicked her stopwatch as Holly finished the weave poles. "That's the fastest ever—you're amazing, Holls!" It was late on Friday afternoon, and Ella and Holly were getting in a quick training session.

The puppy ran to receive her reward—a pat on the head and a crunchy dog biscuit from Ella's pocket.

"Talk about a quick learner!" she said. "And you're not even six months old."

Holly looked up at Ella with her bright brown eyes. She wagged her tail, hoping for another delicious treat.

"Hey!" Ella crouched down to cuddle her beloved puppy. "You've got a couple of new gray speckles on one of your front paws—I'm sure they weren't there before!" Taking Holly's paw, she examined it in detail. "One, two, three, four—they were already there. But these two have just appeared!"

"Talking to yourself?" a voice said as a car door slammed.

"Jen—hi!" Ella was happy to see her mom's assistant. Jen looked nice and relaxed in jeans and a slim-fitting pink shirt. "I thought you weren't due back until tomorrow!"

Holly gave a yip and ran to greet Jen.

"The course finished at lunchtime. And you know me—I can't stay away from Animal Magic a minute longer than I have to!"

"Hi, Jen!" Caleb poked his head out of the reception area door. "Guess what, Ella—three people have made appointments to see Cocoa this weekend."

"Cool!" Jen grinned. "Who's Cocoa?" she asked Ella.

"A beautiful rescue dog. Dad's friend Stephen found her. He saved her life. We already found a home in Ridgewood for the guinea pigs—Billie and Bailey, remember? Plus a perfect home out at Tall Pines Farm for Gypsy!"

"Wonderful!" Jen beamed. She detoured across the yard to visit the pony in the stables. "So someone actually wants to give you a home, you silly monkey!"

She laughed as Gypsy leaned over her door and banged her bony head against Jen's shoulder. "You have such attitude, Gypsy my girl! I only hope your new owners know what they're getting themselves into."

"And Holly's already learned two tests for her agility training!" Ella rushed on with the week's news. "The hoop and the weave poles…."

"Oh, yes, you told me about that." Jen made her way toward the reception area. "It sounds fascinating."

"I'll just take Holly back to the house and join you," Ella continued. She didn't want to miss a scrap of information about Jen's mega-interesting week. "Come on, Holls!"

"…So, in the end, I persuaded her," Caleb told Jen.

It was no good—Ella had been quick, but as she ran into the reception area, she knew she'd missed something important.

"You persuaded who to do what?" she demanded.

"Slow down, Ella," Mom told her through the open door of the examination room, where she was busy identity-chipping Bun-Bun and Bella, the two black-and-white bunnies. "One of these days, you'll bust a gut!"

"I persuaded Mia to come in at lunchtime today to take a look at Bella and Bun-Bun," Caleb told her.

Ella's jaw dropped. "But I heard her say Fern would be jealous, Fern was way too precious, blah-blah!"

"You never knew your brother had a persuasive side, did you, Ella?" Mom put the two rabbits into their cage and carried it into the reception area.

"When did you talk to Mia?" Ella asked.

"Last night, after you and Annie left. We were doing homework, but in the middle of math, I brought up the idea of adopting another rabbit again, and eventually I got through to her."

"She'll let Fern have a friend?" Ella shook her head in amazement. "Hey, Caleb, that's cool. Good job!"

Mom laughed. "Did I hear family harmony just break out?"

"No, honestly." Ella was excited. "We really think that's what's wrong with Fern, don't we? She's lonely. This could be the answer."

"And here come your visitors now, by the look of things," said Jen, who was standing by the window. She watched two people get out of their car in the parking lot. "Is this them?"

Mother and daughter walked into the reception area. Mia looked nervous and hung back on the porch.

Uh-oh! She's about to change her mind! Ella thought.

It was Mrs. Logan who ushered her daughter into the building. "Don't make a decision until you've at least looked at these rescue rabbits," she pleaded.

"I don't think it'll be fair to Fern," Mia muttered, staring at the floor and deliberately not looking at Caleb. "She wouldn't be happy, Mom."

"Just take a quick look," Caleb said. "Bun-Bun and Bella are right here."

Yes, take a look! Ella willed Mia to love Bun-Bun and Bella as much as she did.

"But only if you want to," Jen said

75

calmly. "We definitely don't want to force you to adopt these rabbits."

"To be honest, I'll try anything," Mrs. Logan confided in Jen and Mom as Mia reluctantly stepped forward to peer into the cage. "The entire household is upset over this. First it's Fern who won't settle in her new home. Then it's Mia moping and making herself sick with worry. Now my husband is grumbling and saying he wishes we'd never moved to a new house in the first place since it's caused so much trouble."

Mia looked in and saw two sweet black-and-white faces. Bella's nose had a long white stripe down the middle, while Bun-Bun's was pure black. Bella had one white ear and one black. Bun-Bun twitched a pair of snowy white ears. "Oh!" Mia exclaimed. "How cute!"

"They're both really tame," Caleb assured her. "Would you like to hold one?"

Mia frowned and held back, so Ella rushed in. She opened the cage and lifted Bella up. "Since they've been here with us, we've handled them at least twice a day to keep them friendly," she explained, tipping Bella onto her back and tickling her tummy. "Mom says they're Netherland dwarfs—you can tell by their short ears and cute round faces. See how she likes being tickled?"

"They've both been vaccinated and spayed," Mom told Mrs. Logan quietly. "And I'd just finished identity-chipping them as you came in."

"Well?" Mia's mom asked, studying her daughter's serious face.

"They're both really sweet," Mia admitted. She glanced up at Caleb. "Is it okay if I hold Bun-Bun?"

Beautiful and soft and silky! Ella thought, crossing her fingers as Mia took Bun-Bun in her arms. *And look at those huge brown eyes! Who could resist!*

"Bun-Bun and Bella are about the same size as Fern," Mia said, softly rubbing Bun-Bun's head.

"Yes, and since they're a dwarf variety, they won't grow any bigger," Mom said.

"Do you know what kind of home
Bella and Bun-Bun came from?" Mia
asked. She handed Bun-Bun back to
Caleb, then gently took Bella from Ella.

Mom shook her head. "They were
found in a garbage can in a restaurant
parking lot about five miles away. The
building owner brought them here."

Mia gasped. "How horrible! You mean
somebody just threw them away?"

In the background, Ella gave Caleb a
grin.

He smiled back.

"That's so cruel!" Mia insisted,
cuddling Bella close to her chest.

"They so need a new home!" Ella
whispered. Life had been pretty tough
for Bella and Bun-Bun. How could you
not take pity on them and love them?

"There definitely would be room in Fern's new hutch," Mia said quietly.

"Does that mean 'yes'?" Mrs. Logan prompted. She seemed eager to get Mia to make a decision.

Mia tickled Bella under the chin, then turned to look at Bun-Bun's sweet, black face.

"Fern would make friends with her, wouldn't she?" she asked Jen.

"It might take her a day or two to get used to a companion, but yes, she'd love to have company, I'm sure."

"So which one would you like to bring home?" Mrs. Logan asked. "Bella or Bun-Bun?"

Ella and Caleb saw a look of doubt flicker across Mia's face. Bella or Bun-Bun? Bun-Bun or Bella? Black-faced Bun-Bun with the pure white bib and white front paws? Or Bella with the flash of white down her face and the band of white around her tummy?

"That's hard," Mia whispered. "What

will happen to Bun-Bun if I choose Bella?"

"We'll find Bun-Bun a good home with a different family," Mom promised.

"But won't Bella miss Bun-Bun if we separate them?" Mia asked. "I bet they've been together ever since they were born."

Choose both! Ella had been keeping her fingers crossed for a long time now. *Not Bun-Bun or Bella, but Bun-Bun and Bella!*

There was a long silence, interrupted only by Mia's soft sighs.

"Well?" Mom asked at last.

"We can hardly leave one behind, can we?" Mrs. Logan said to break the tension.

Mom, Jen, Caleb, and Ella all smiled

in relief.

"Okay, so let's take them both," Mia's mom said. "Come along, Bella and Bun-Bun. Come home with us and meet Fern!"

Chapter Seven

A Worrisome Phone Call

In the kennels the following morning, Ella brushed Cocoa's smooth, shiny brown coat. "We have to make you look extra pretty," she told her. "A lot of people are coming to see you today!"

The rescue dog wagged her long, thin tail. Her ears were pricked, and her head was tilted to one side.

As Caleb popped his head around the door, a dozen dogs began a chorus of excited barks. "Is Cocoa ready yet?" he yelled.

"Almost!"

"The first appointment is at nine-thirty."

Caleb came down the row of kennels to inspect Cocoa. "That's enough brushing, Ella," he said. "She looks fine

to me."

"See how well the cut on her paw healed." Cocoa was one of Ella's favorites, and she found an excuse to spend a few extra minutes with her before the first group of potential owners arrived. "You did a great job yesterday, Caleb—with Mia, I mean. I never would've thought she'd go for the companion rabbit idea."

Caleb blushed. "Thanks. I've taken Bun-Bun and Bella off the website."

"Don't change the subject!" Ella teased. "Mia must really trust you."

"Yeah, well, fingers crossed it all works out," he muttered as Jen came into the kennels.

"The first person to see Cocoa is here," she announced, to another round of sharp barks.

"Is it a couple—Mr. and Mrs. Harvey?" Caleb asked, putting Cocoa on the leash.

Jen shook her head. "It's a man. He didn't give his name."

So Caleb and Ella went with Cocoa into the reception area. "Stephen!" Ella gasped when she saw her dad's coworker standing there.

"What's up?" Caleb asked as Cocoa recognized her rescuer and wagged her tail. "We weren't expecting you."

Stephen looked embarrassed. "Maybe I should have called."

"If you came to see how Cocoa is doing, you're just in time," Ella told him.

She let the dog off the leash and

smiled as she trotted up to Stephen.

"Hello there, girl." Stephen bent down
to pet her. "I must say, you're looking
a whole lot better than when I found
you!"

Cocoa licked his hand and wagged
her tail some more.

"She's saying thanks!" Caleb laughed.

"So you found her a good home?"
Stephen asked awkwardly. "Is that
what you meant about me arriving just
in time?"

Caleb was about to tell him about the
three appointments they had lined up
for Cocoa, starting with Mr. and Mrs.
Harvey, but Ella stepped in quickly.
"Not exactly," she told Stephen. "Why
do you ask?"

Stephen cleared his throat. "The thing
is—I've been talking to my girlfriend
all week about it, and she's finally said
yes. I didn't mention it to your dad
in case it led nowhere. But now that
Cheryl has agreed—"

"—you want to adopt Cocoa
yourself!" Ella jumped in.

"That's right—I do." Stephen kneeled down and put his arms around Cocoa's neck. The dog covered his face in grateful licks.

Ella grinned at the surprise turn of events. "Wow, that's cool! It's totally cool!"

"So Caleb called the people who had been interested in meeting Cocoa and persuaded them to come and look at the other dogs. And Stephen adopted Cocoa! He took her away on the spot!" Ella told Annie as they constructed a seesaw for Holly's agility training. Annie had placed an empty plastic paint can on its side

in the middle of the Animal Magic
yard, and now Ella was carefully
balancing a long plank of wood
across it.

Yip! Yip! Holly ran in crazy circles
around the yard.

"Are you sure this will work?"
Annie asked as she tested the wobbly
seesaw.

"Of course it will. Anyway, Stephen
lives next to a park in Ridgefield, so
Cocoa will get plenty of walks. You
should've seen how happy she was to
go with him to her new home."

In the background, Ella could hear
the phone ringing in the reception
area. It was lunchtime, and she knew
there was no one there to answer
it. "Keep an eye on Holls, will you,

Annie?" she asked as she ran indoors.

"Hello, Animal Magic, Ella
speaking," she said as she picked up the
receiver.

"Oh, thank goodness. Please come
quickly!" a girl's voice said.

"I'm sorry, we usually ask people
to bring their pets in to the Rescue
Center."

It took Ella a second or two to recognize
Mia, and she felt her heart lurch. "Mia—
what is it? What's wrong?"

Mia was sobbing so hard she could
barely speak. "It's Fern. Oh, I should
never have done it. I knew something
bad would happen!"

"What's the matter? Has she been in
a fight with Bun-Bun and Bella?" Ella
asked.

It was less than 24 hours since Mia and her mom had taken the rabbits home, and already there was a crisis.

"No. It's worse than that. Someone has to come—please!"

"Okay, okay, listen, Mia." Ella tried to think straight. "You're saying something's wrong with Fern?"

"Yes. She's been sick, and now she's gone all limp. I brought her into the house as soon as I realized...."

"Mom's not here, but Jen is. She's in the cat area. I'll ask her to come to the phone."

"No, tell her to come right over here," Mia begged. "And tell her to be quick, please, Ella, before it's too late!"

Jen grabbed her medical kit, and she and Ella ran across Main Street and up Three Oaks Road to the Logans' house.

Mrs. Logan was waiting at the front door. "Thank you for coming," she told them. "Mia's so upset."

Jen and Ella followed Mrs. Logan through the house. They found Mia kneeling in the sunroom, bending over her precious Fern, who lay on a white towel on the floor.

"She's really, really sick!" Mia sobbed, her eyes red and her face streaked with tears. "This is how I found her in her hutch—just lying there."

Jen nodded. "Let's lift her up onto this table. That's it—gently. Now let's take a look at her. You say she's been sick, but did she have diarrhea, too?"

Mia shook her head.

Ella felt a tight knot of worry form in
her stomach—poor Fern didn't react,
even when Jen felt her abdomen and
examined her eyes and mouth.

"It's possible that she's picked up an infection," Jen commented. "She's certainly dehydrated. Mrs. Logan—do you have a small plastic dropper we could use to drip some liquid into her mouth?"

As Mrs. Logan dashed off to the medicine cabinet and Mia continued to sob, Ella glanced out the sunroom window.

She saw the long wire run built by Mr. Logan and the magnificent new hutch at the far end of the yard.

"Bun-Bun and Bella have made Fern sick!" Mia cried. "They had a bug, and they gave it to her!"

"No, that's not true," Ella objected. "Bella and Bun-Bun didn't have any bugs—they were totally healthy all the time they were at Animal Magic."

But Mia shook her head. "They're the reason Fern's sick. They gave her a bug, and now she's going to die!"

"It's okay," Jen said. "No one's going to die if we can possibly help it."

"It's all your fault, Ella," Mia wept. Tears streamed down her cheeks as Mrs. Logan returned with the dropper. "I never would have let those two rabbits near Fern if it hadn't been for you!"

Chapter Eight

The Search

Ella stepped out of the sunroom door onto the lawn. She felt breathless with worry and was upset that Mia had blamed Bella and Bun-Bun for making Fern sick, but she knew that if anyone could figure out what was wrong with Mia's beloved rabbit, Jen could.

A breeze blew through the still-bare trees in the woods behind the Logans' yard, making Ella shiver and zip up her fleece. She crouched beside the rabbit hutch to check how Bella and Bun-Bun

had settled in. *That's funny*, she thought.
The door to the bedroom should be closed!

But it was hanging open, and on the
feeding platform the water bottle was
dripping clear liquid onto the dish of oats
that Mia had put down earlier.

"Bella? Bun-Bun? Where are you?"
Ella called, reaching carefully inside the
dark bedroom and finding to her dismay
that it was empty. She looked under the
ramp and into the shaded area behind—
nothing!

"Mia!" she cried, jumping up and
running back down the lawn toward the
house. Her heart thumped as she checked
the empty run. "I've got some awful
news—Bun-Bun and Bella have escaped!"

"Caleb, I think Mia left the hutch door open on purpose." Ella spoke quickly into her phone as she stood alone on the pavement outside the Logans' house. "She didn't act surprised when I told her that Bella and Bun-Bun had run away."

"Are you sure they're not in the hutch?" Caleb asked. He and Annie had offered to come and help, and they were on their way up Three Oaks Road as he spoke. "Look again, Ella, just to make sure."

"They're not there!" she insisted, spotting him and Annie at the bottom of the hill. "Mia thinks our Animal Magic rabbits made Fern sick, but that's not true. Jen says she'll take a blood sample to find out what's wrong. Hurry up, you two—we have to set up a search party and find Bun-Bun and Bella!"

"Calm down, Ella," Caleb said, hanging up as he and Annie ran up the hill. "You didn't go accusing Mia of letting them escape on purpose, did you?" he asked when he reached the house.

Ella shook her head. "But honestly—that's what it looks like. Mia would never leave the hutch door open by mistake. She's much too careful for that."

"Even though she's worried crazy about Fern?" Annie reminded her. All three were hurrying up the Logans' driveway, crossing paths with Jen as they reached the front door.

"I got the blood sample," Jen told them. "I'm going straight into Ridgefield, to the lab, to get it processed as quickly as possible."

"Does Mom know?" Ella asked.

Jen nodded. "I called her, and she's heading back to hold down the fort. I take it you three are going to look for Bella and Bun-Bun?"

"We'll start in the backyard," Caleb

told her. "Where's Mia? Is she with Fern?"

"Yes. I've told her to keep Fern warm and give her plenty of water."

"Let's go down the side of the house," Annie suggested, wanting to avoid Mia so they could get on with the search.

So she, Ella, and Caleb skirted the house and spread out across the backyard, looking under bushes and behind a bench, turning over big empty flowerpots and a watering can to see if Bun-Bun and Bella were hiding there.

"Let's try behind the greenhouse," Caleb suggested. He pushed around some old leaves, pricking himself on the thorns of a rose bush climbing up the fence. "Ouch!" he said, sucking his finger as it began to bleed.

Annie sighed and shook her head.

"They've vanished into thin air," she muttered. A sudden thought struck her as she gazed at the breeze-blown thicket beyond the fence. "You don't think..." she began.

"...that Bun-Bun and Bella got out of the yard and into the woods?" Ella gasped. She pictured the stout tree trunks and rough, rocky ground that went on for what seemed like miles to the distant hilltop. "If they did, we'll never find them!"

"Maybe not, but we can try," Caleb said stubbornly, pulling at the latch on the gate. "Come on!"

He dashed ahead and Annie followed him, while Ella ran back to the hutch and grabbed the dish of oats. *Just in case*, she thought, though her hopes weren't high as she followed Caleb and Annie into the woods.

The ground spread out before her— bright yellow daffodils poking out of the dark earth, new green shoots coming through everywhere she looked. Overhead, the bare tree branches made crisscross patterns across the bright blue sky.

"Caleb, Annie—where are you?" Ella yelled.

"I'm down by the stream," Caleb called back. "Annie went straight ahead, along the trail. You go up the hill, Ella, so we're spread out."

She set off with the dish of food, trying not to crush the daffodils underfoot, bending down to search behind mossy stones and under fallen branches. "Here, Bella! Here, Bun-Bun!" she whispered. She spotted what looked like a rabbit hole to the right, and then another—in fact, an entire warren. Of course, the woods would be teeming with wild rabbits, and they wouldn't take kindly to two black-and-white strangers. Tame animals never did well in the wild, Ella knew. Her heart thumped more loudly than ever.

"Anything?" Caleb yelled from the bank of the stream.

"Nothing!" Annie and Ella both yelled back.

Ella climbed farther up the hill. She stopped when she thought she heard a rustling in the undergrowth. "Crow," she muttered as the bird broke cover and flew up into a tree. She tiptoed on up the hill.

"Still nothing!" Annie reported from way below. "We're never going to find them!"

"Keep trying!" Caleb said.

Ella reached the top of the hill, where the trees were thinner and green grass grew. She glanced back down the daffodil-covered slope. Out of the corner of her eye, Ella spotted movement under a nearby bush and a flash of black-and-white. She froze.

The grass parted and Bella appeared, hopping uncertainly, then sitting back on her hind legs to twitch her ears and nose, staying still as a statue when she spotted Ella.

Still Ella didn't move a muscle. Did Bella recognize her? Did she know she was a friend?

There was another rustle in the bush and Bun-Bun hopped clear, her dark eyes shining, the white marking under her chin bright in the shadow of the trees.

"It's me," Ella whispered. Slowly, slowly she bent her knees until she was low enough to place the dish of food on the ground. "Remember me? I'm not going to hurt you," she promised.

Bun-Bun and Bella stared at her. They seemed very small out in the big world, and very scared.

"I know—you don't belong out here," Ella whispered. "You've seen scary squirrels and crows. There are wild versions of you everywhere."

The two rabbits stared, twitching their whiskers and smelling the oats in the dish. They listened to Ella's soft, familiar voice.

Slowly they hopped toward her.

"Nice food," Ella said. "Yummy!"

Hop-hop. Bella came first. She flicked her ears, then ducked her head toward the dish. Hop. Bun-Bun joined her. The oats smelled good, and they tasted even better.

"And this is where I pick you up," Ella whispered. Gently she stretched out and put a firm hand under Bun-Bun's tummy. She lifted her up and tucked her under her right arm, reaching out for Bella at the same time, then holding her close.

The rabbits were soft and warm. They didn't struggle.

"I've got them!" Ella called to Caleb and Annie. "They're both fine. We're coming down."

Chapter Nine

Finally, Some Answers

Back in the Logans' yard, Caleb knocked on the sunroom door.

Mrs. Logan opened it and invited them in.

"Mia, we found Bun-Bun and Bella for you," Caleb said, frowning as he saw her sitting on the floor beside Fern, who was wrapped in the white towel and lying very still.

Annie and Ella stood outside the door, holding the two black-and-white rabbits in their arms.

"Mia, did you hear what Caleb said?" Mrs. Logan prompted.

Mia looked up with a blank expression.

"I don't care," she whispered. "I don't want them anymore."

Ella gasped. "But...," she began.

"They gave Fern a horrible bug!" Mia wailed. "Look how sick she is!"

This wasn't fair, so Ella spoke out. "No, listen—Fern was sick before Bella and Bun-Bun came, remember?"

"There's no point, Ella," Mrs. Logan sighed. "At the moment, Mia's too upset about Fern to listen to what you're saying."

So Caleb backed out of the sunroom, and together he, Annie, and Ella took Bella and Bun-Bun back to Animal Magic.

"Mia just turned her back on them," Annie explained to Mom. "It's like they were birthday presents that she didn't want."

Ella was close to tears. She'd let Caleb return the two rabbits to the small animals unit. "It's not fair," she told her mom.

"How could our rabbits have made Fern sick? Mia brought Fern in for you to look at way before Bella and Bun-Bun ever went near her!"

"People who love their animals and who are upset when they get sick don't always make a lot of sense," Mom reminded them. "Are you okay, Caleb?" she asked as he came back into the reception area. "You're not feeling too bad about things, are you?"

Quickly, Caleb shook his head and went out into the yard to greet Jen, who had just gotten back from Ridgefield.

"It's a shame," Mom said. "But there really is nothing we can do about it."

Caleb burst back into the room a moment later. "Jen's got Fern's blood results," he told them excitedly.

Annie and Ella crowded around Jen as she showed Mom the printout.

"Severe anemia—which means she's low in iron—and a vitamin deficiency," Jen reported. "Mia's rabbit has not been receiving a balanced diet."

Mom studied the results with a puzzled look. "But Mia's the last person in the world to neglect Fern's diet. If anything, we all agree she's given her a lot of attention."

"Exactly!" Jen felt she'd hit on the answer. She turned to Ella, Caleb, and Annie. "Tell me in detail—what does Mia feed her rabbit?"

"Fresh fruit," Annie answered.

"Raw vegetables," Ella said. "And she lets her graze the grass in her run."

"Oats," Caleb added.

Jen listened carefully. "And that's what she's always given her?"

They nodded. "Nothing but the best," Caleb insisted.

"Then I think Fern has been getting away with what's called selective feeding," Jen explained. "We concentrated on it in part of the course this week. It's when a pet like a rabbit or a hamster is given a loose cereal feed and is able to pick out bits of food that they prefer and discard the rest. The owner might not notice it, but it means that over time, the pet misses out on essential nutrients."

"Like toddlers only eating sweet, sugary stuff and pushing away food that's actually good for them," Mom realized.

"So how could Mia have prevented it?" Caleb asked.

"By feeding Fern nuggets instead of loose cereal. The nuggets are made by crushing all the ingredients together and forming little pellets. That way, the pet swallows everything it needs."

"And that's what's happened to Fern?" Ella asked. "Selective feeding? Would she be this sick if she was low in—what was it—iron and vitamins?"

Mom and Jen nodded. "Definitely, if it happened over a long period of time," Mom said.

"And can you help Fern get better?" Annie asked anxiously.

"For sure," Jen told them in a confident voice. "Caleb, pick up the phone and tell Mia to bring Fern down here right away!"

Chapter Ten
A Happy Ending

"Fern's unbalanced diet has made her prone to gastrointestinal problems," Jen explained to Mrs. Logan.

"That's stomach problems to you and me," Caleb told Mia.

Jen, Mrs. Logan, Caleb, and Mia were in the examination room with Fern. Ella, Annie, and Mom looked in through the open door.

"That's why she was lethargic and started vomiting," Jen went on as she gave Fern vitamins from a dropper. "Without the blood test, we might never have put our finger on the problem."

"So it was my fault that Fern was sick?" Mia said in a small voice. "Not anybody else's—just mine?"

"You couldn't have known," Ella told her. "It takes an expert like Jen or Mom to come up with the answer."

"But I blamed you," Mia sighed as tears welled up in her eyes. She petted Fern while Jen worked. "I'm sorry, Ella, and Caleb, too—I shouldn't have said those things."

"What things?" Caleb kidded, shrugging his shoulders and giving Mia a quick smile. "Don't even worry about it."

"Please watch Fern for a sec," Mia whispered to him, turning and going over to Ella. "I'm sorry I blamed Bella and Bun-Bun and sent them back here. I wasn't thinking straight."

"That's okay." Ella's reaction was stiffer than Caleb's. Even though the crisis was over and Fern was going to get better, she still couldn't quite forgive Mia.

"And one other thing," Mia went on, looking straight into Ella's eyes. "I know you probably think I left the hutch door open and let Bun-Bun and Bella escape on purpose, but I didn't."

Ella looked steadily back at Mia.

"I was in a panic," Mia explained. "Fern had just gotten sick, and she was lying on her side, all lifeless, so I just grabbed her and ran for the house. I forgot all about the door."

Slowly, Ella nodded. "I believe you," she replied. And a great weight seemed to lift from her mind.

"Come back tomorrow for Bun-Bun and Bella," Mom had told the Logans. "Settle Fern back into her hutch overnight, keep her warm, and make sure she has plenty to drink."

So it was arranged for three o'clock on Sunday afternoon, which turned out to be a beautiful spring day with a blue sky and a crisp breeze.

"Hoop!" Ella told Holly. They were out in the yard putting in a bit of training.

The puppy galloped at the green

plastic ring and leaped straight through.

"Good girl—now, weave poles!"

In and out of the line of sticks Holly raced.

"Hooray!" Annie and Jen clapped from the side of the yard. "Great job, Holly!"

"Now, seesaw!" Ella called out.

Brave little Holly trotted toward one end of the plank. She stepped on it and got her balance, then she ventured to the middle, feeling the plank tilt and violently dip.

"Whoa, steady!" Dad cried.

"Cool!" Ella beamed as Holly kept her balance and completed the seesaw just as she had taught her. Ella called Holly to her for a pat and a biscuit treat. "You're doing great, Holls!"

"Absolutely!" Jen agreed.

They were so busy congratulating
their wonder-pup that they didn't
notice Mia walk into the yard until
Caleb took a step back and bumped
right into her.

"Oh, I'm sorry!" he gasped, then
blushed.

"I forgive you." She grinned. "I came to take Bella and Bun-Bun home. Is that okay?"

"They're in a pet carrier in the reception area waiting for you," Ella told Mia eagerly.

She was about to run and get them when her dad grabbed her arm.

"What?" Ella asked.

Dad nodded toward Caleb. "Let him do it," he said quietly.

"Oh—right!" Ella got it at last. She stood back to watch Caleb lead Mia into Animal Magic.

Soon they came back out with Bun-Bun and Bella in the carrier. "I'll help you carry them up the hill," Caleb offered.

It was Mia's turn to blush. "Thanks,"

she replied, letting Caleb lead the way across the yard.

"How's Fern?" Jen asked as Mia followed Caleb through the gate.

"Much better already, thanks!" Mia told her. "I think she's looking forward to seeing Bun-Bun and Bella again."

"I'm glad," Jen said quietly.

And the small group came together in the middle of the yard at Animal Magic to watch Caleb and Mia cross Main Street and carry the two rescue rabbits up Three Oaks Road to their new home.

"Isn't that exactly what we do here?" Mom said. She'd come up behind Dad, Ella, Annie, and Jen as Mia and Caleb had left the yard. "We work our magic to match the perfect pet..."

"...with the perfect owner!" they chorused.

"Isn't it great when it works out?" Ella sighed.

"Couldn't be better," her dad agreed.

"Which is why we're having the Animal Magic party next weekend," Mom reminded them. "To say thank you to everyone, and to look forward to the next 12 months. Let's hope they're as good as the last."

"That's right! The party!" Annie and Ella cried.

"Can we have a barbecue?" Ella pleaded, her eyes sparkling. "Please, please, please? Burgers and hot dogs and ketchup, with paper plates. We could set it up by the house, and people can go inside for drinks from the fridge...."

Yip! Holly agreed with a lively wag
of her tail. When it came to food, she
knew what she liked. Definitely hot
dogs, please!